For the man who really does have Yes
Days with his grandkids—my dad
—A.K.R.

Thanks to Cramer-Krasselt, for the
inspiration, and to my wife, Jan, for
twenty-five years of yeses
—T.L.

kook productions
amy krouse rosenthal & tom lichtenheld

Yes Day!
Text copyright © 2009 by Amy Krouse Rosenthal
Illustrations copyright © 2009 by Tom Lichtenheld
Manufactured in China.
Library of Congress Cataloging-in-Publication Data
Rosenthal, Amy Krouse.
  Yes Day! / Amy Krouse Rosenthal & Tom Lichtenheld. — 1st ed.
    p. cm.
  Summary: A little boy gets everything he asks for on Yes
Day, a special day that only comes once a year.
  ISBN 978-0-06-115259-7 (trade bdg.) — ISBN 978-0-06-
115260-3 (lib. bdg.)
  [1. Wishes—Fiction. 2. Day—Fiction.] I. Lichtenheld, Tom.
II. Title.
PZ7.R719445Ye 2009   2008020219
[E]—dc22   CIP
                                                            AC

Typography by Jeanne L. Hogle
1 2 3   4 5 6 7 8 9 10
❖
First Edition

Today is my
FAVORITE
day of the year!

YES DAY!

Amy Krouse Rosenthal & Tom Lichtenheld

HarperCollinsPublishers

Just watch, you'll see what I mean. . . .

Can I please have pizza for breakfast?

Can I use
your hair gel?

Can I clean my room
tomorrow?

Can I pick?

Can we get ice cream?

Can I eat lunch outside?

Can we have a food fight?

Can we invent our own game?

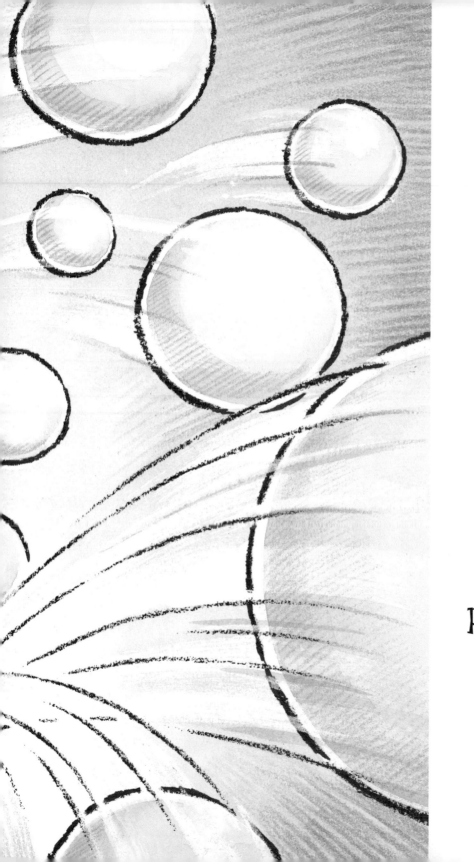

Can I have a
piggyback ride?

Can Mario come
over for dinner?

Can we stay up *really* late?

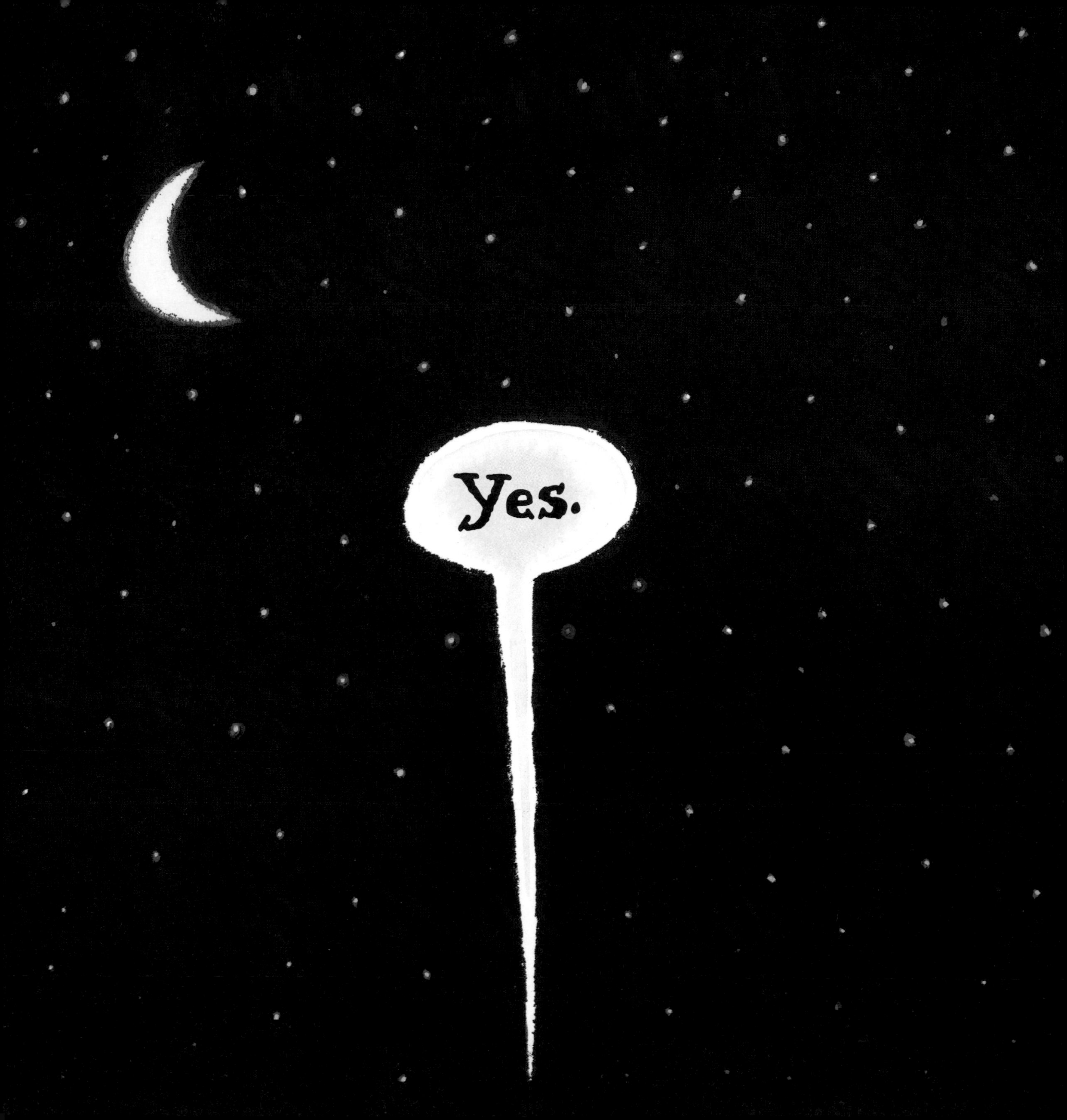
Yes.

The End
(of Yes Day)

See you again next year!